Tales Of A
Gambling Grandma

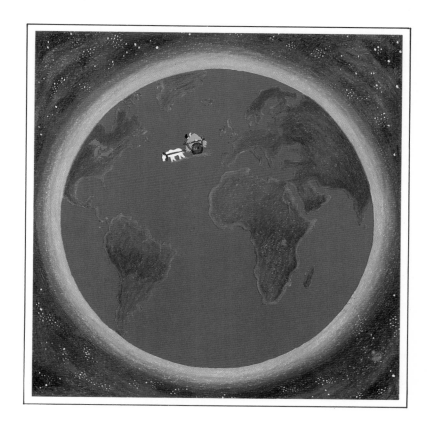

Text and Pictures by Dayal Kaur Khalsa

CLARKSON N. POTTER, INC./PUBLISHERS
DISTRIBUTED BY CROWN PUBLISHERS, INC., NEW YORK

My grandma was a gambler. This is the story of her life as she told it to me and as I remember it.

Grandma was born in Russia. When and where exactly, she did not know. She only remembered that one night the Cossacks charged into her village, brandishing their swords and scaring all the people.

My grandma (who was only three years old) jumped into a cart full of hay and covered herself. Somewhere she lost her shoe. And so, she escaped to America wearing only one little black shoe, hiding in a hay cart drawn by a tired white horse, all the way across the wide, slate-green Atlantic Ocean. At least, that's how she told the story to me.

She landed in Brownsville, Brooklyn.

There she grew up.

When she was old enough to get married, my grandma borrowed a balalaika. She couldn't play the balalaika, but she could hum very loudly.

Every evening she sat down with her balalaika on the front steps of her building, trying to catch a husband.

One night, Louis the plumber, trudging home weary from work, saw her. She made such a pretty picture with her balalaika and her long golden hair and rosy cheeks that he dropped his heavy leather bag of plumbing tools—*clank*—and asked her to marry him.

And she, actually strumming the balalaika—*plink, plank, plunk*—said, "Yes."

And that's how our family began.

They had two children.

My grandpa got a job fixing the pipes in Dutch Schultz's hideout. Dutch Schultz was a big-time gangster, and though he broke the law a lot, he was very kind to my grandpa. He paid him lots of money and always gave it to him on time.

But good jobs like that were hard to find. To help make extra money, my grandma learned how to play poker.

She was very good—sharp-eyed and quick with her hands. She could mark a card with her finger-nail and hide aces in her sleeve. And, most important, she liked to win. Wherever there was a hot card game going on in Brooklyn, my grandma was there—winning money.

Her children grew up.

Her son moved out to California. Her daughter (who was my mother) married a handsome man from Queens. They bought a brand-new house.

When my grandpa died, my grandma moved into their house in Queens. Then, I was born; a pink little girl for her to hug and squeeze.

My parents worked all day, so right from the start my grandma and I were always together.

We spent most of our time under the great weeping willow tree in our front yard. My grandma sat like a flowering mountain in her big green garden chair. All day long she knit scarfs and shawls and socks. She told me stories of her life and gave me two important pieces of advice.

One: Never, ever go into the woods alone because the gypsies will get you or, should you escape
that cruel fate, you'll fall down a hole.

Two: Just in case the Cossacks come to Queens,
learn to say "*Da*" and always keep plenty of borscht
in the refrigerator.

Whenever I had a cold, Grandma let me stay in her bed. She made a tent from a sheet and an overturned chair. All day long we kept busy together polishing pennies bright copper.

When I became bored with this, she'd slowly slide open her bedside table drawer.

I liked that drawer.

First there was the smell of sweet perfume and musty old pennies. Then there was a tiny dark blue bottle of Evening in Paris cologne, shaped like a seashell; a square snapshot of my grandma holding me as a baby; big, thick, wriggly legged black hairpins; and stuck in corners so I had to use the hairpins to get them out, dull brown dusty pennies.

But most fascinating of all were my grandma's false teeth. I never saw her put them in her mouth. She always kept them in the drawer, or if she were going visiting, they stayed smiling secretly in the pocket of her dress.

My grandma let me touch everything, even the teeth.

And she'd promise if I would get better really fast, she'd take me somewhere.

To the midway at Coney Island.

To a vaudeville show, starring Rosie, the Beer-Drinking Hippopotamus.

To a movie that had the very same name as my
grandma—*Anna.*

Or to a Chinese restaurant, where we drank tea in thick little cups.

Grandma had lived a very long time, she said, and she had learned a thing or two.

Sometimes, as I grew older, she would look at me in a certain way and say, "Let me give you a few friendly words of advice." This was always followed by what she called "A Law of Life."

One law was all about how to draw people: Always color their cheeks bright pink and give them big red smiles so they look healthy.

Another law was about crossing your eyes: Don't—because the cords will snap and they'll stay that way forever.

And whenever I had a question but there was no answer right away, Grandma told me her very best Law of Life: "Don't worry. Sooner or later, for every pot there's a lid."

Most of our time was spent quietly under the willow tree, just the two of us. There were occasional visitors under our willow tree—other children in a quiet mood, the next-door cat on its way somewhere else, the mailman, and two tall nuns who lived around the corner.

And every Thursday afternoon the Sunshine
Ladies came.

Grandma missed the excitement of her old gambling days, so she organized the other grandmas in the neighborhood into the Sunshine Ladies Card Club. They met in our backyard.

At first they played canasta just to win pennies. Then, to make it more interesting, my grandma suggested they play for what she called "trifles"—gold lipstick cases, compacts, pillboxes, charms, brooches, lockets—anything that was shiny and gold.

My grandma won everything.

E very year Grandma took a long train trip
straight out across the country to California to
visit her son. She traveled on the Santa Fe Chief.

And that train was so luxurious, she said, that she
spent the whole trip soaking in a big white tub full
of fresh orange juice.

When she arrived in California, "Bright orange," she said, her son picked her up at the train station and brought her to his little pink stucco bungalow. He arranged a giant-sized, two-week-long poker game in her honor.

All his friends came. They played poker, chewed gum, ate potato chips, and drank celery tonic without end. My grandma had a wonderful time.

And she brought back a fabulous prize she had won in the poker game. It was a big bright shiny gold ring with two glittering diamond chips.

She let me hold the ring for a while and told me that when I grew up it would be all mine. Then she dropped the heavy ring into a little green velvet bag and put it in her bedside table drawer with the other treasures.

It was just around then that Grandma decided it was time for me to learn how to play cards. After supper one night Grandma cleared the dining room table quickly. She lined up little piles of pennies and set out a fresh deck of cards. She taught me how to play go fish, old maid, and gin rummy.

At first we played just to win those dusty pennies brought down from her drawer.

But after a few weeks of lessons, when I had learned how to hold my cards close to my chest so no one could see them, and to *not* bounce up and down yelling "Guess what I have!" every time I got a good hand—then she taught me how to play what she called "*real* cards"—straight poker, five-card stud, three-card monte, chicago, and blackjack.

Grandma kept using the old pennies from her drawer. I used my allowance. "To make it more interesting," my grandma suggested.

Grandma wiped me out.

Any part of my allowance that I hadn't lost playing poker, I put in a shoebox in the bottom of my closet. I was saving up to buy a Ping-Pong-Pow Gun, a giant plastic bazooka that shot real ping-pong balls.

I saved and saved and saved and at last I had enough money to buy the gun.

Grandma took me downtown to Macy's toy department. I rushed to the Ping-Pong-Pow display and grabbed a gun. My grandma picked up a pink-cheeked Betsy-Wetsy doll.

She had the same look on her face as when she had warned me about the gypsies and the Cossacks and the holes. She looked down at my giant bazooka and slowly shook her head. "Let me give you a few friendly words of advice," she said. "Guns are for boys. Girls play with dolls. Buy the doll."

I had never disagreed with my grandma before. But—a doll!

"No!" I said. "Anyone can play with anything!"

And that was the only real argument my grandma and I ever had.

Guess who won?

Every day I came home from school for lunch. Grandma sat waiting for me at the dining room table.

I only ate sandwiches that were cut into four long pieces with the crusts cut off. My grandma understood this because her favorite sandwich was a banana rolled up in a piece of rye bread. I never sat down to eat. Instead, while my grandma listened to the soap operas on the big brown radio, I marched around and around the living room rug, stepping only on the roses. Every once in a while, I'd make a loop into the dining room to take another tiny sandwich from my grandma's outstretched hand.

One day Grandma got sick. Her eyes turned bright yellow and my parents took her to the hospital.

When I came home for lunch the door was locked. A neighbor called to me, saying my mother said I should have lunch at her house.

I sat in a chair in her silent kitchen, with no soap opera, and ate a sandwich cut only in two. Then I went back to school.

When I came home at three o'clock the front door was open. I went into the house and into the darkened dining room. My mother was sitting at the table.

She said, "I have something very sad to tell you."

And I said, "Yes?"

And she said, "Your grandma died this afternoon."

And I said what I had heard other people say sometimes: "Oh, I'm sorry to hear that." And I went upstairs to my grandma's room.

I opened the drawer of her treasures and made sure that everything was there: the pennies, the bottle of cologne, the snapshot, her hairpins and false teeth, and the little bag with the ring.

Then I opened her closet door and stepped inside. I closed the door behind me and hugged and smelled all my grandma's great big dresses.

And that's the story of my grandma's life as she told it to me and as I remember it.

When I grew up, my mother gave me my grandma's gold and diamond ring. And though I found out that it wasn't made out of real gold at all and that the diamond chips were only glass, I wouldn't trade my grandma's ring for all the gold and diamonds in the world.

For all the Khalsa children

Published by Clarkson N. Potter, Inc., 225 Park Avenue South, New York, New York 10003.

CLARKSON N. POTTER, POTTER, and colophon are trademarks of Clarkson N. Potter, Inc.

Manufactured in Belgium

Library of Congress Cataloging-in-Publication Data
Khalsa, Dayal Kaur.
Tales of a gambling grandma.

Summary: Reminiscences of a grandmother who came to this country from Russia, married a plumber, gambled to earn extra money, and formed a strong bond with her young granddaughter.
[1. Grandmothers—Fiction] I. Title.
PZ7.K52647Tal 1986 [Fic] 85-28126

ISBN 0-517-56137-9

10 9 8 7 6 5 4 3 2 1

First Edition

Notable Books 1986